*Frictions*

August Strindberg



Translation by Ellie Schleussner

NOVELLIX
— *stories to go* —

www.novellix.se

Originally published in Swedish in *Giftas* by
Albert Bonniers Förlag, Sweden, 1884

Original title: *Slitningar*
Translation: Ellie Schleussner

12

Design: Lisa Benk
Print: Livonia Print, Riga, 2025
ISBN: 978-91-7589-222-1

MIX
Paper | Supporting responsible forestry
FSC® C002795
FSC
www.fsc.org

HIS EYES HAD BEEN OPENED. He realised the perversity of the world, but he lacked the power to penetrate the darkness and discover the cause of this perversity; therefore he gave himself up to despair, a disillusioned man. Then he fell in love with a girl who married somebody else. He complained of her conduct to his friends, male and female, but they only laughed at him. For a little while longer he trod his solitary path alone and misunderstood. He belonged to "society", and joined in its pursuits, because it distracted him; but at the bottom of his heart he had nothing but contempt for its amusements, which he took no pains to conceal.

One evening he was present at a ball. He danced with a young woman of unusual beauty and animation. When the band ceased playing, he remained standing by her side. He knew he ought to talk to her but he did not know what to say. After a while the girl broke the silence.

"You are fond of dancing, Baron?" she said with a cold smile.

"Oh no! Not at all," he answered. "Are you?"

"I can't imagine anything more foolish," she replied.

He had met his man, or rather his woman.

"Why do you dance, then?" he asked.

"For the same reason that you do."

"Can you read my mind?"

"Easily enough; if two people think alike, the other always knows."

"H'm! You're a strange woman! Do you believe in love?"

"No!"

"Nor do I! You and I ought to get married."

"I'm beginning to think so myself."

"Would you marry me?"

"Why not? At any rate, we shouldn't fight."

"Horrible idea! But how can you be so sure?"

"Because we think alike."

"Yes, but that might become monotonous. We should have nothing to talk about, because the one would always know what the other is thinking."

"True; but wouldn't it be even more monotonous if we remained unmarried and misunderstood?"

"You are right! Would you like to think it over?"

"Yes, until the cotillion."

"No longer?"

"Why any longer?"

He took her back to the drawing room and left her there, drank several glasses of champagne and watched her during supper. She allowed two young members of the Diplomatic Corps to wait on her, but made fun of them all the time and treated them as if they were footmen.

As soon as the cotillion began, he went to her and offered her a bouquet.

"Do you accept me?" he asked.

"Yes," she replied.

And so they were engaged.

It's a splendid match, said the world. They are made for one another. They are equals as far as social position and money are concerned. They hold the same blasé views of life. By blasé the world meant that they cared very little for dances, theatres, bazaars, and other noble sports without which life is not really worth living.

They were like carefully wiped twin slates, exactly alike; but utterly unable to surmise whether or not life would write the same legend on both. They never asked one another during the tender moments of their engagement: Do you love me? They knew quite well that it was impossible, because they did not believe in love. They talked little, but they understood one another perfectly.

And they married.

He was always attentive, always polite, and they were good friends.

When the baby was born, it had but one effect on their relationship; they had something to talk about now.

But by-and-by the husband began to reveal a certain energy. He had a sense of duty, and moreover, he was sick of being idle. He had a private income, but was in no way connected with politics or the Government. Now he looked round for some occupation which would fill the void in his life. He had heard the first morning call of the awakening spirits and felt it his duty to do his share of the great work of research into the causes of human misery. He read much, made a careful study of politics and eventually wrote an article and sent it to a paper. The consequence was that he was elected a member of the Board of Education. This necessitated hard reading in future, for all questions were to be threshed out thoroughly.

The Baroness lay on the sofa and read Chateaubriand and Musset. She had no faith in the improvement of humanity, and this stirring up of the dust and mould which the centuries had deposited on human institutions irritated her. Yet she noticed that she did not keep pace with her husband. They were like two horses at a race. They had been weighed before the start and been found to be of the same weight; they had promised to keep side by side during the run; everything was calculated to make them finish the race and leave the course at the same time. But already the husband had gained by the length of a neck. Unless she hurried up, she was bound to be left behind.

And the latter really happened. In the following year he was made controller of the budget. He was away for two months. His absence made the Baroness realise that she loved him; a fact which was brought home to her by her fear of losing him.

When he returned home, she was all eagerness; but his mind was filled with the things he had seen and heard abroad. He realised that they had come to the parting of the ways, but he would have liked to delay it, prevent it, if possible. He showed her in great living pictures the functioning of the colossal gigantic machinery of the State, he tried to explain to her the working of the wheels, the multifarious transmissions, regulators and detents, unreliable pendulums and untrustworthy safety valves.

She was interested at first, but after a while her interest waned. Conscious of her mental inferiority, her insignificance, she devoted herself entirely to her baby, anxious to demonstrate to her husband that she yet had a value as a model mother. But her husband did not appreciate this value. He had married her for the sake of companionship, and he found in her an excellent nurse for his child. But how could it be helped now? Who could have foreseen such a thing?

The house was always full of members of Parliament, and politics was the subject of conversation at dinner. The hostess merely took care that no fault could be found with the cooking. The Baron never omitted to have one or two men amongst his guests who could talk to his wife about music and the drama, but the Baroness wanted to discuss nothing but the nursery and the bringing up of children. After dessert, as soon as the health of the hostess was drunk, there was a general stampede to the smoking room where the political discussions were continued. The Baroness left her guests and went to the nursery with a feeling of bitterness in her heart; she realised that her husband had so far outdistanced her that she could never again hope to come up with him.

He worked much at home in the evening; frequently he was busy at his writing table until the small hours of the morning, but always behind locked doors. When he noticed afterwards, as he sometimes did, that his wife went about with red eyes, he felt a pain in his heart; but they had nothing to say to each other.

Occasionally however, at those times when his work palled, when he realised that his inner life was growing poorer and poorer, he felt a void within him, a longing for warmth, for something intimate, something he had dreamed of long ago, in the early days of his youth. But every feeling of that sort he suppressed at once as unfaithfulness to his wife, for he had a very high conception of the duty of a husband.

To bring a little more variety into her daily life, he suggested one day that she should invite a cousin of whom she had often spoken, but whom he had never seen, to spend the winter with them in town.

This had always been a great wish of the Baroness's, but now that the realisation of it was within her power, she changed her mind. She did not want her in the least now. Her husband pressed her for reasons, but she could not give him any. It roused his curiosity and finally she confessed that she was afraid of her cousin; afraid that she might win his heart, that he might fall in love with her.

"She must be a queer girl, we really must have her here!"

The Baroness wept and warned, but the Baron laughed and the cousin arrived.

One afternoon the Baron came home, tired as usual; he had forgotten all about the cousin and his curiosity in regard to her. They sat down to dinner. The Baron asked the cousin if she was fond of the theatre. She replied that she was not. She preferred reality to make-believe. At home she had founded a school for black sheep and a society for the care of discharged prisoners. Indeed! The Baron was much interested in the administration of prisons. The cousin was able to give him a good deal of information, and during the rest of the dinner the conversation was exclusively about prisons. Eventually the cousin promised to treat the whole question in a paper which the Baron was going to read and work up.

What the Baroness had foreseen, happened. The Baron contracted a spiritual marriage with the cousin, and his wife was left out in the cold. But the cousin was also beautiful, and when she leaned over the Baron at his writing desk, and he felt her soft arm on his shoulder and her warm breath against his cheek, he could not suppress a sensation of supreme wellbeing. Needless to say, their conversation was not always of prisons. They also discussed love. She believed in the love of the souls, and she stated as plainly as she could, that marriage without love was prostitution. The Baron had not taken much interest in the development of modern ideas on love, and found that her views on the subject were rather hard, but after all she was probably quite right.

But the cousin possessed other qualities, too, invaluable qualifications for a true spiritual marriage. She had no objection to tobacco smoke for instance, in fact, she was very fond of a cigarette herself. There was no reason, therefore, why she should not go into the smoking-room with the men after dinner and talk about politics. And then she was charming.

Tortured by little twinges of conscience, the Baron would every now and then disappear from the smoking room, go into the nursery, kiss his wife and child, and ask her how she was getting on? The Baroness was grateful, but she was not happy. After these little journeys the Baron always returned to his friends in the best of tempers; one might have thought that he had faithfully performed a sacred duty. At other times it irritated and distressed him that his wife did not join the party in the smoking room, too, as his wife; this thought was a burden which weighed quite heavily on him.

The cousin did not go home in the spring, but accompanied the couple to a watering place. There she organised little performances for the benefit of the poor, in which she and the Baron played the parts of the lovers. This had the inevitable result that the fire burst into flames. But the flames were only spiritual flames; mutual interests, like views, and, perhaps, similar dispositions.

The Baroness had ample time to consider her position. The day arrived when she told her husband that since everything was over between them, the only decent thing to do was to part. But that was more than he had bargained for; he was miserable; the cousin had better return to her parents, and he would prove to his wife that he was a man of honour.

The cousin left. A correspondence between her and the Baron began. He made the Baroness read every letter, however much she hated doing it. After a while, however, he gave in and read the letters without showing them to his wife.

Finally the cousin returned. Then matters came to a crisis. The Baron discovered that he could not live without her.

What were they to do? Separate? It would be death. Go on as at present? Impossible! Annul the marriage which the Baron had come to look upon as legal prostitution and marry his beloved? However painful it might be, it was the only honest course to take.

But that was against the wishes of the cousin. She did not want it said of her that she had stolen another woman's husband. And then the scandal! The scandal!

"But it was dishonest not to tell his wife everything; it was dishonest to allow things to go on; one could never tell how the matter would end."

"What did he mean? How could it end?"

"Nobody could tell!"

"Oh! How dared he! What did he think of her?"

"That she was a woman!"

And he fell on his knees and worshipped her; he said that he did not care if the administration of prisons and the school for black sheep went to the devil; he did not know what manner of woman she was; he only knew that he loved her.

She replied that she had nothing but contempt for him, and went helter-skelter to Paris. He followed at her heels. At Hamburg he wrote a letter to his wife in which he said that they had made a mistake and that it was immoral not to rectify it. He asked her to divorce him.

And she divorced him.

A year after these events the Baron and the cousin were married. They had a child. But that was a fact which did not interfere with their happiness. On the contrary! What a wealth of new ideas germinated in their minds in their voluntary exile! How strong were the winds which blew here!

He encouraged her to write a book on "young criminals". The press tore it to pieces. She was furious and swore that she would never write another book. He asked her whether she wrote for praise, whether she was ambitious?—She replied by a question: Why did he write?—A little quarrel arose. He said it was refreshing to hear her express views which did not echo his own—always his own.—Always his own? What did he mean? Didn't she have views of her own? She henceforth made it her business to prove to him on every occasion that she was capable of forming her own opinions; and to prevent any errors on his part she took good care that they always differed from his. He told her he did not care what views she held as long as she loved him.—Love? What about it? He was no better than other men and, moreover, he had betrayed her. He did not love her soul, but her body.—No, he loved both, he loved her, every bit of her!—Oh! How deceitful he had been!—No, he had not been deceitful, he had merely deceived himself when he believed that he loved her soul only.

They were tired of strolling up and down the boulevard, and sat down before a cafe. She lighted a cigarette. A waiter requested her rather uncivilly, not to smoke. The Baron demanded an explanation and the waiter said that the cafe was a first-class establishment and the management was anxious not to drive away respectable people by serving these ladies. They rose from their seats, paid and went away. The Baron was furious, the young Baroness had tears in her eyes.

"There they had a demonstration of the power of prejudice! Smoking was a foolish act as far as a man was concerned, but in a woman it was a crime! Let him who was able to do so, destroy this prejudice! Or, let us say, him who would care to do so! The Baron had no wish that his wife should be the first victim, even if it were to win for her the doubtful honour of having cast aside a prejudice. For it was nothing else. In Russia, ladies belonging to the best society smoked at the dinner table during the courses. Customs changed with the latitudes. And yet those trifles were not without importance, for life consisted of trifles. If men and women shared bad habits, intercourse between them would be less stiff and formal: they would make friends more easily and keep pace with one another. If they had the same education, they would have the same interests, and cling together more closely during the whole of their lives."

The Baron was silent as if he had said something foolish. But she had not been listening to him; her thoughts had been far away.

"She had been insulted by a waiter, told that she was not fit to associate with respectable people. There was more behind that, than appeared on the surface. She had been recognised. Yes, she was sure of it, it was not the first time that she had noticed it."

"What had she noticed?"

"That she had been treated with little respect at the restaurants. The people evidently did not think that they were married; because they were affectionate and civil to one another. She had borne it in silence for a long time, but now she had come to the end of her tether. And yet this was nothing compared to what they were saying at home!"

"Well, what were they saying? And why had she never told him anything about it before?"

"Oh! Horrible things! The letters she had received! Leaving the anonymous ones quite out of the question."

"Well, and what about him? Was he not being treated as if he were a criminal? And yet he had not committed a crime! He had acted according to all legal requirements, he had not broken his marriage vows. He had left the country in compliance with the dictates of the law; the Royal Consistory has granted his appeal for a divorce; the clergy, Holy Church, had given him his release from the bonds of his first marriage on stamped paper; therefore he had not broken them! When a country was conquered, a whole nation was absolved from its oath of loyalty to its monarch; why did society look askance at the release from a promise? Had it not conferred the right on the Consistory to dissolve a marriage? How could it dare to assume the character of a judge now and condemn its own laws? Society was at war with itself! He was being treated like a criminal! Hadn't the secretary of the Embassy, his old friend, on whom he had left his and his wife's cards, acknowledged them by simply returning one card only? And was he not overlooked at all public functions?"

"Oh! She had had to put up with worse things! One of her friends in Paris had closed her door to her, and several had cut her in the street."

"Only the wearer of a boot knew where it pinched. The boots which they were wearing now were real Spanish boots, and they were at war with society. The upper classes had cut them. The upper classes! This community of semi-imbeciles, who secretly lived like dogs, but showed one another respect as long as there was no public scandal; that was to say as long as one did not honestly revoke an agreement and wait until it had lapsed before one made use of one's newly-regained freedom! And these vicious upper classes were the awarders of social position and respect, according to a scale on which honesty ranked far below zero. Society was nothing but a tissue of lies! It was inexplicable that it hadn't been found out long ago! It was high time to examine this fine structure and inquire into the condition of its foundations."

They were on friendlier terms on arriving home than they had been for many years. The Baroness stayed at home with her baby, and was soon expecting a second one. This struggle against the tide was too hard for her, and she was already growing tired of it. She was tired of everything! To write in an elegantly furnished, well-heated room on the subject of discharged prisoners, offering them, at a proper distance, a well-gloved hand, was a proceeding society approved of; but to hold out the hand of friendship to a woman who had married a legally divorced man was quite another thing. Why should it be so? It was difficult to find an answer.

The Baron fought in the thick of the battle. He visited the Chamber of Deputies, was present at meetings, and everywhere he listened to passionate diatribes against society. He read papers and magazines, kept a keen eye on literature, studied the subject deeply. His wife was threatened by the same fate which had overtaken the first one; to be left behind! It was strange. She seemed unable to take in all the details of his investigations, she disapproved of much of the new doctrine, but she felt that he was right and fighting for a good cause. He knew that he could always count on her never-flagging sympathy; that he had a friend at home who would always stand by him. Their common fate drove them into each other's arms like frightened birds at the approach of a storm. All the womanliness in her,—however little it may be appreciated now-a-days,—which is after all nothing but a memory of the great mother, the force of nature which is woman's endowment, was roused. It fell on the children like the warm glow of a fire at eventide; it fell on the husband like a ray of sunshine; it brought peace to the home. He often wondered how it was that he did not miss his old comrade, with whom he was wont to discuss everything; he discovered that his thoughts had gained force and vigour since he stopped pouring them out as soon as he conceived them; it seemed to him that he was profiting more by the silent approval, the kindly nod, the unwavering sympathy. He felt that his strength had increased, that his views were less under outside control; he was a solitary man, now, and yet he was less solitary than he had been in the past, for he was no longer constantly met by contradictions which merely filled his heart with misgivings.

It was Christmas Eve in Paris. A large Christmas tree, grown in the wood of St. Germain, stood in their little chalet on the Cours de la Reine. They were going out after breakfast to buy Christmas presents for the children. The Baron was pre-occupied, for he had just published a little pamphlet, entitled: "Do the Upper Classes constitute Society?" They were sitting at breakfast in their cosy dining room, and the doors which led to the nursery stood wide open. They listened to the nurse playing with the children, and the Baroness smiled with contentment and happiness. She had grown very gentle and her happiness was a quiet one. One of the children suddenly screamed and she rose from the table to see what was the matter. At the same moment the footman came into the dining room with the morning post. The Baron opened two packets of printed matter. The first was a "big respectable" newspaper. He opened it and his eyes fell on a headline in fat type: "A Blasphemer!"

He began to read: "Christmas is upon us again! This festival dear to all pure hearts, this festival sacred to all Christian nations, which has brought a message of peace and goodwill to all men, which makes even the murderer sheathe his knife, and the thief respect the sacred law of property; this festival, which is not only of very ancient origin, but which is also, especially in the countries of the North, surrounded by a host of historic associations, etc., etc. And then like foul fumes arising from a drain, an individual suddenly confronts us who does not scruple to tear asunder the most sacred bonds, who vomits malice on all respectable members of society; malice, dictated by the pettiest vengeance...." He refolded the paper and put it into the pocket of his dressing gown. Then he opened the second parcel. It contained caricatures of himself and his wife. It went the same way as the first, but he had to be quick, for his wife was re-entering the dining room. He finished his breakfast and went into his bedroom to get ready to go out. They left the house together.

The sunlight fell on the frosted plane trees of the Champs Elysées, and in the heart of the stony desert the Place de la Concorde opened out like a large oasis. He felt her arm on his, and yet he had the feeling as if she were supporting him. She talked of the presents which they were going to buy for the children, and he tried to force himself to take an interest in the subject. But all at once he interrupted her conversation and asked her, à-propos of nothing:

"Do you know the difference between vengeance and punishment?"

"No, I've never thought about it."

"I wonder whether it isn't this: When an anonymous journalist revenges himself, it is punishment; but when a well-known writer, who is not a pressman, fights with an open visor, meting out punishment, then it is revenge! Let us join the new prophets!"

She begged him not to spoil Christmas by talking of the newspapers.

"This festival," he muttered, "on which peace and goodwill..."

They passed through the arcades of the Rue de Rivoli, turned into the boulevards and made their purchases. They dined at the Grand Hotel. She was in a sunny frame of mind and tried to cheer him up. But he remained preoccupied. Suddenly he asked,

"How is it possible that one can have a bad conscience when one has acted rightly?"

She did not know.

"Is it because the upper classes have so trained us, that our conscience troubles us whenever we rebel against them? Probably it is so. Why shouldn't he who has been hurt unjustly, have the right to attack injustice? Because only he who has been hurt will attack, and the upper classes hate being attacked. Why did I not strike at the upper classes in the past, when I belonged to them? Because, of course, I didn't know them then. One must look at a picture from a distance in order to find the correct visual point!"

"One shouldn't talk about such things on Christmas Eve!"

"True, it is Christmas. This festival of..."

They returned home. They lit the candles on the Christmas tree; it radiated peace and happiness; but its dark branches smelt of a funeral and looked sinister, like the Baron's face. The nurse came in with the little ones. His face lighted up, for, he thought, when they are grown up they will reap in joy what we have sown in tears; then their conscience will only trouble them when they have sinned against the laws of nature; they won't have to suffer from whims which have been caned into us at school, drummed into us by the parsons, invented by the upper classes for their own benefit.

The Baroness sat down at the piano when the maids and the footmen entered. She played melancholy old dances, dear to the heart of the people of the North, while the servants danced gravely with the children. It was very much like the penitential part of divine service.

After that the presents were distributed among the children, and the servants received their gifts. And then the children were put to bed.

The Baroness went into the drawing-room and sat

down in an armchair. The Baron threw himself on a footstool at her feet. He rested his head on her knees. It was so heavy—so heavy. She silently stroked his forehead. "What! Was he weeping?"

"Yes!"

She had never before seen a man weep. It was a terrible sight. His big strong frame shook, but he made no sound.

"Why was he weeping?"

"Because he was unhappy."

"Unhappy with her?"

"No, no, not with her, but still, unhappy."

"Had anybody treated him badly?"

"Yes!"

"Couldn't he tell her all about it?"

"No, he only wanted to sit at her knees, as he used to sit long ago, at his mother's."

She talked to him as if he had been a child. She kissed his eyes and wiped his face with her handkerchief. She felt so proud, so strong, there were no tears in her eyes. The sight of her inspired him with new courage.

"How weak he had been! That he should have found the machine-made attacks of his opponents so hard to bear! Did his enemies really believe what they said?"

"Terrible thought! Probably they did. One often

found stones firmly grown into pine trees, why should not opinions grow into the brain in the same way? But she believed in him, she knew that he was fighting for a good cause?"

"Yes, she believed it! But—he must not be angry with her for asking him such a question—but—did he not miss his child, the first one?"

"Yes, certainly, but it could not be helped. At least, not yet! But he and the others who were working for the future would have to find a remedy for that, too. He did not know, yet, what form that remedy would take, but stronger brains than his, and many together, would surely one day solve this problem which at present seemed insolvable."

"Yes, she hoped it would be so."

"But their marriage? Was it a marriage in the true sense of the word, seeing that he couldn't tell her what troubled him? Wasn't it, too, pro...?"

"No, it was a true marriage, for they loved one another. There had been no love between him and his first wife. But he and she did love one another, could she deny it?"

"She couldn't, he was her dear love." Then their marriage was a true marriage before God and before Nature.

SHORT STORIES PUBLISHED BY NOVELLIX

N°1 Virginia Woolf *Lappin and Lapinova*
N°2 D.H. Lawrence *Sun*
N°3 Katherine Mansfield *Bliss*
N°4 Charles Dickens *Horatio Sparkins*
N°5 Astrid Lindgren *Most Beloved Sister & Mirabelle*
N°6 August Strindberg *Frictions*
N°7 Selma Lagerlöf *The Silver Mine*
N°8 Stig Dagerman *Sleet*
N°9 Håkan Nesser *How I Spend My Days and My Nights*
N°10 Karin Tidbeck *Anywhere Out of the World*
N°11 Arne Dahl *Migraine*
N°12 Henning Mankell *The Man on the Beach*
N°13 Oscar Wilde *The Nightinggale and the Rose...*
N°14 Mary Shelley *The Trial of Love*
N°15 Leo Tolstoy *After the Dance*
N°16 Virginia Woolf *The Legacy*
N°17 Karen Blixen *The Pearls*
N°18 Henrik Pontoppidan *The Grim Reaper*
N°19 Herman Bang *Irene Holm*
N°20 H.C. Andersen *Little Claus and Big Claus*
N°21 Selma Lagerlöf *The Legend of the Christmas Rose*
N°22 Charles Dickens *A Christmas Carol – Stave one*
N°23 Louisa May Alcott *A Christmas Dream*
N°24 H.C. Andersen *The Fir Tree*
N°25 Virginia Woolf *Kew Gardens*
N°26 James Joyce *The Boarding House*
N°27 Edith Wharton *The Quicksand*
N°28 Katherine Mansfield *The Garden Party*
N°29 Marcel Proust *The Melancholy Summer of Madame de Breyves*
N°30 Honoré de Balzac *A Street of Paris and Its Inhabitant*
N°31 Gustave Flaubert *The Legend of Saint Julian the Hospitaller*
N°32 Guy de Maupassant *Paul's Mistress*

*Most Beloved Sister*

*Mirabelle*

Astrid Lindgren

Translation by Linda Schenck

NOVELLIX
— *stories to go* —

www.novellix.com

Original titles: *Allrakäraste syster* & *Mirabell*

First published in 1949 in *Nils Karlsson-Pyssling* by
Rabén & Sjögren, Sweden.
Published by arrangement with Rabén & Sjögren
and Astrid Lindgren AB, Sweden.

For more information regarding the works of
Astrid Lindgren, please contact info@astridlindgren.se.

6

Translation: Linda Schenck
Design: Lisa Benk
Livonia Print, Riga, 2025
ISBN: 978-91-7589-572-7

FSC
www.fsc.org
MIX
Paper | Supporting
responsible forestry
FSC® C002795

## *Most Beloved Sister*

NOW I'D LIKE to tell you a secret no one knows but me. *I've got a twin sister.* Don't tell anybody! Not even my mother and father know. Long ago when my sister and I were just born, this was seven years ago, my sister ran right out and hid behind the big rosebush at the back of our yard. Imagine, she could run so far when she was newly born!

Do you want to know my sister's name? I'm sure you think it's Lena or Birgitta or one of those regular girls' names. But it's not, not a bit. Her name is Ylva-lee. Say it a few times in a row and you'll hear how pretty it sounds: Ylva-lee Ylva -lee, Ylva-lee.

Me, I'm just called Barbara. But Ylva-lee never says my name. She calls me "Most Beloved Sister."

Ylva-lee is very fond of me. Father is fondest of

Mother and Mother is fondest of my baby brother, who was born last spring. But Ylva-lee cares for me alone.

It was a hot day yesterday. Early in the morning I went to sit behind the rosebush, as usual. It's in a corner of the yard where no one ever goes. Ylva-lee and I have a special language no one but we understand. The rosebush is called something completely else in our language. It's called Salikon. Sitting there behind Salikon, I heard Ylva-lee call out to me:

"Ceem har!"

That's how you say "come here" in our language. So I crawled down into the hole.

There's a hole in the ground right under Salikon. I crawled in there. Then I climbed down the long, long ladder and passed through the dark passage all the way to the door leading to the Golden Chamber, where Ylva-lee is queen. I thumped on the door.

"Is that my Most Beloved Sister?" I heard Ylva-lee say from inside.

"Yes," I replied.

"Nicko, please open for my Most Beloved Sister," said Ylva-lee.

Then the door opened and Nicko, the little dwarf

who cooks for Ylva-lee, bowed and beamed, as he always does. Ylva-lee and I gave each other big, long hugs. And then Ruff and Duff came rushing at us, yapping and jumping. Ruff and Duff, they're our little black poodles.

Ruff is mine and Duff is Ylva-lee's. Ruff always gets so excited when I arrive. He licks my hands and wags his tail and is just so cute. I always used to nag at Mother and Father about getting me a dog. But they just said dogs were too expensive and too much trouble and not good for my baby brother, besides. That's why I was so pleased to have Ruff. We played with our dogs for a long time, Ylva-lee and I, and had lots of fun. Then we went to feed our rabbits. We've got a whole slew of little white rabbits.

You really can't imagine how beautiful the Golden Chamber is. The walls glitter with gold, and in the middle of the room is a fountain full of lovely green water. Ylva-lee and I often swim there.

After we fed the rabbits, we decided to ride. Ylva-lee's horse is white. His mane is gold and his hooves are gold. My horse is black. His mane and his hooves are silver. Our horses are called Goldfoot and Silverfoot.

We rode through the Big Bad Woods where The Evil Ones live. The Evil Ones have green eyes and long arms. They came rushing after us. They didn't speak. They didn't shout. Just ran silently behind our horses extending their long arms toward us. The Evil Ones wanted to capture us and put us in the Big Bad Cave. But Goldfoot and Silverfoot ran so fast sparks flew from their hooves. Golden sparks and silver sparks. The Evil Ones fell farther and farther behind.

We rode out onto the meadow where the Kind Ones live. The Evil Ones can't go there. They have to stay in the Big Bad Woods. They stayed at the edge of the woods peering between the trees with their scary green eyes.

We had so much fun with the Kind Ones. We dismounted from our horses and sat down in the meadow. Goldfoot and Silverfoot rolled in the meadow too, neighing. The Kind Ones wear soft white clothes and have rosy cheeks, and they served us delicious cookies and sweets from green trays. No other sweets are as good as the sweets the Kind Ones serve. Right in the middle of the meadow the Kind Ones have a great big stove. That stove is where they make their sweets and bake their cookies.

Next we rode to the Loveliest Dale in the World. No one but Ylva-lee and I can go there. The flowers sing and the trees play music. There's a clear little stream running through the dale. It cannot sing or play music, but it hums a melody. Never have I heard a prettier melody.

Ylva-lee and I were standing on the bridge across the little stream listening to the singing of the flowers and the music of the trees and the humming of the stream with its melody. That was when Ylva-lee held my arm ever so tight and said:

"Most Beloved Sister, there is one thing you must know!"

My heart just ached when she said that.

"No," I said. "I don't want to know."

"Well, it's important that you know," Ylva-lee went on.

At that moment the flowers stopped singing and the trees played no more music, nor could I hear the melody of the stream.

"Most Beloved Sister," said Ylva-lee. "When the roses of Salikon wither, I shall be dead."

I jumped up onto my horse and rode away, tears streaming down my cheeks. I rode as fast as I could. Ylva-lee came rushing behind on her horse. We rode so fast Goldfoot and Silverfoot were drenched in sweat by the time we were back in the Golden Chamber.

Nicko had made us such wonderful pancakes. We sat on the floor in front of the fireplace and ate them.

Ruff and Duff jumped around us. Our rabbits came hopping over too, and joined in.

In the end I had to go home. Ylva-lee accompanied me to the door. We gave each other great big farewell hugs.

"Come back soon, Most Beloved Sister," said Ylva-lee.

I walked out the door and along the passageway and up the ladder. I heard Ylva-lee call out to me once more:

"Come back soon, Most Beloved Sister."

When I walked into the nursery, Mother was putting my baby brother to sleep. Her face was very pale, and the moment she set eyes on me she tossed my baby brother into his crib and rushed to me. She took me in her arms, weeping, and said:

"My darling child, where have you been? Where have you been all day?"

"Behind the rosebush," I replied.

"Oh thank goodness, thank goodness you're here now," said Mother and kissed me.

"We've been beside ourselves with worry,"

Then she said:

"You'll never guess what Father brought home for you today!"

"No, what?"

"Look in your room," said Mother.

I ran to my room as fast as I could. And there, in a basket by my bed, was a little black poodle puppy, fast asleep. Soon he woke up and jumped around barking. He was the cutest dog I've ever seen in my whole life, even cuter than Ruff down in the Golden Chamber. He was somehow more alive, he really was.

"He's yours and yours alone," said Mother.

I picked him up and held him in my arms, and he barked and tried to lick my face. He really was the cutest dog I have ever seen.

"He's called Ruff," said Mother.

Now wasn't that strange?

I loved Ruff and I was so happy I could hardly sleep that night. Ruff lay in his basket alongside my bed. Now and then he whined a little in his sleep.

Ruff is mine and mine alone.

This morning when I went out into the yard, I could see that all the roses of Salikon had withered. And there was no more hole in the ground.

## *Mirabelle*

Now I'm going to tell you about the most amazing thing that's ever happened in my whole life. It was two years ago. I was only six years old back then. Now I'm eight.

My name is Britta-Kaisa. But my name doesn't really matter. My mother and father and I live in a tiny little house with a small yard. Our house is very secluded. No one else lives nearby. Outside our yard a narrow little road runs, and at the end of that road – far away – is a town. My father is a gardener. Every Wednesday and Saturday he drives to town to sell flowers and vegetables at the market square. He is paid for them, but not very much.

My mother says she absolutely cannot make ends meet. In those days – two years ago – all I wanted and I wanted it very, very, *very* badly, was a doll. Sometimes on market days I went along to town with my parents. There's a big toy store at the market square. Every time I was near that store I would stand gazing at all the dolls and wishing *very* hard that I could buy one of them. But Mother would say it was quite impossible, since all the money Father got for his vegetables had to go to food and clothes and other things we needed. I could see there was no hope of getting my own doll, but I just couldn't stop *wishing*.

Now I'm coming to the amazing part. One spring day two years ago Mother and Father had gone to the market square to sell cowslips and birch shoots. I stayed home, who knows why? But it was lucky I did! Early that evening, as dusk started to fall, I went into the yard to listen, thinking I might hear them coming down the hill.

It was such an odd evening. The whole yard and our house and the road twisting and turning; everything looked odd. There was just something odd in the air, well, I can't find the words to tell you how odd it was. Just as I was standing there looking down the road, I heard a horse and buggy approaching, and I got very happy thinking Mother and Father were on their way home. But it wasn't them. It was an odd little man driving around the bend. I waited in the yard, watching his buggy come closer and closer. In the end I shook myself into action and ran out to open the gate so he wouldn't have to get down. There's a gate across the road quite close to our house, you see, and I often open it for drivers as they approach. Sometimes they give me a coin. When I opened for that odd little man, I was a little bit frightened since I was all alone and far from any neighbours and I couldn't know whether or not he was a kind man. But he looked kind. When he had passed through the gate he drew his horse in, stopped, looked at me and chuckled. Then he said:

"I really ought to give you a coin for opening. But I don't have one. So here's something else instead. Hold out your hand!"

So I did. And then that odd little man put a little yellow seed into my hand. It shone bright as gold.

"Just plant this seed in your garden and give it a healthy drink of water every day, and you'll see, something you'll be glad for will come up," he said.

Then he cracked his horsewhip in the air and in a very few minutes the cart had passed out of sight and disappeared. I just stood there for ages listening to the rolling of the wheels as the horse vanished into the distance. It was all so very odd.

In the end I went back into our yard and planted his seed in my own little patch of garden behind the house. Then I went in and got my little green watering can and gave the soil where I had planted the seed a good, healthy drink.

Every day for ages and ages I went out and watered, ever so curious to see what would sprout. I thought it might be a rosebush or some other pretty plant. But never ever in my life would I have guessed what *really* came up.

One morning when I came out to water my garden as usual, I saw something red sticking up out of the ground, a little, little corner of something red. The red thing got bigger and bigger by the day, until you could finally tell what it was. Guess what? It was a red doll's hat growing in my garden patch. Now isn't that amazing? You can imagine how much I watered it! I watered morning, noon and night, so Mother and Father said:

"Good grief, sweetie, what a lot of watering! Radishes don't really need that much!"

But they never went and looked, because my garden patch is a bit out of the way.

One morning you could see the whole doll's head. It was the kind of doll who could open and close her eyes, and hers were shut.

She was the most beautiful doll I'd ever seen. She had fair, curly hair under the red hat, and pink cheeks and a red mouth.

After some time her whole body had come up. She had such a terribly cute red dress made of the same fabric as her hat. Once she was out up to her knees I asked Mother and Father to come see what was growing in my patch. I suppose they expected just to find radishes and spinach but still they came. And never have I seen such surprise on their faces as when they saw that doll. They just stood there staring for ages. Then Father said:

"Well I never!"

And Mother said:

"What on earth is this all about?"

"Well, it's about me planting a doll seed in this earth," I said.

And Father said he wished he'd had a whole bushel of those doll seeds, so he could sell lots and lots of dolls at the market, because they would bring in more money than radishes. For the rest of the day, Mother and Father just went around astonished.

Then guess what? One Sunday morning when I went out to my patch, my doll had just finished growing. On her feet she had pretty white socks and little white leather shoes. I sat down on the grass just to admire how pretty she was. And then – at that very moment – she opened her eyes and looked straight at me. She had blue eyes, just as I had expected. I'd never seen a more wonderful doll, and I couldn't keep from patting her. But when I did that, she broke right off at the root. Yes, there was a root under her feet. Right then I knew she was meant to be mine. So I picked her up. I ran straight to show her to Mother and Father.

And then I took her to my room and made her a little cradle out of the hood of Mother's sewing machine, since I didn't have a dolly bed for her. I played with her all day, and I was so happy I could hardly eat. I named her Margareta. When bedtime came, I settled her right down in her sewing machine cradle and said:

"Good night, Margareta."

And you'll never guess what happened! Well, my doll opened her mouth and said:

"My name isn't Margareta! Wherever did you get that from? I'm Mirabelle."

Can you imagine, she could talk! She babbled on and on, and I was so amazed I couldn't even reply. She told me she wanted a real bed of her own and a nightgown. And then she told me she liked me very much and wanted me to be her mother.

"But never try giving me porridge," she said, "because I don't eat porridge."

I needed some time to think so I crept down into my own bed and lay there without saying a word. Mirabelle was quiet too. But soon I could see why she wasn't saying anything – she was trying to climb up onto my dresser. And she did it, too! Once she was up on the dresser she jumped down into her bed, I mean into the hood of the sewing machine. She did this over and over again, giggling with pleasure, and she said:

"I must say, this is really fun!"

A few minutes later, she came over to my bed. Tilting her head, she asked:

"May I come up and lie with you there? You're my mother now."

I lifted her up into my bed and she lay there and chattered. I loved listening to her. I was so happy about Mirabelle, the happiest I have ever been in my whole life. In the end she stopped talking. After yawning a couple of times – such very cute yawns – she lay her head in the crook of my arm and fell asleep. I didn't have the heart to move her. I just let her sleep there all night. It took me a very long time to fall asleep, but I just lay there listening to her breathing in the dark.

The next morning when I woke up, Mirabelle had

climbed up onto the little table by my bedside. There was a glass of water on it. Mirabelle poured out all the water. Then she laughed and jumped down into the hood of the sewing machine. Mother came in to wake me a few minutes later and found Mirabelle lying there looking just like an ordinary doll.

Now I've had Mirabelle for two years. And I don't think any other little girl in all the world has such a wonderful doll as my doll. She's a bit difficult sometimes, I admit. But I still like her ever so much. No one but me knows she can talk and laugh and eat just like a regular person. When Mother or Father is nearby she stares straight ahead and doesn't look a bit alive. But when we're alone – well, you should see her. We have so much fun! She loves little doll pancakes. I have a doll pancake skillet and I make her pancakes every day.

Mother thinks I just pretend Mirabelle can eat. But she eats for real. Once she bit my finger, just in fun of course. Father made a bed for her, so she doesn't have to lie in the sewing machine hood any more. Mother made sheets and a quilt. And I've sewed her a pretty little nightgown, some pinafores, and an everyday dress. Mirabelle loves it every time she gets something new. I play with her all day long except when I have to help Father weed the garden.

Every time I hear a horse and buggy on the road I rush down to the gate to see if it might be the odd little man coming back. I would very much love to thank him for my beautiful, beautiful doll. But it's never him.

Would you like to see my doll, my beautiful, sweet Mirabelle? Come pay me a visit and I'll show her to you. Just follow the narrow little road that leads to our house. I promise to be waiting by the gate with Mirabelle.

SHORT STORIES PUBLISHED BY NOVELLIX

N°1 Virginia Woolf *Lappin and Lapinova*
N°2 D.H. Lawrence *Sun*
N°3 Katherine Mansfield *Bliss*
N°4 Charles Dickens *Horatio Sparkins*
N°5 Astrid Lindgren *Most Beloved Sister & Mirabelle*
N°6 August Strindberg *Frictions*
N°7 Selma Lagerlöf *The Silver Mine*
N°8 Stig Dagerman *Sleet*
N°9 Håkan Nesser *How I Spend My Days and My Nights*
N°10 Karin Tidbeck *Anywhere Out of the World*
N°11 Arne Dahl *Migraine*
N°12 Henning Mankell *The Man on the Beach*
N°13 Oscar Wilde *The Nightinggale and the Rose...*
N°14 Mary Shelley *The Trial of Love*
N°15 Leo Tolstoy *After the Dance*
N°16 Virginia Woolf *The Legacy*
N°17 Karen Blixen *The Pearls*
N°18 Henrik Pontoppidan *The Grim Reaper*
N°19 Herman Bang *Irene Holm*
N°20 H.C. Andersen *Little Claus and Big Claus*
N°21 Selma Lagerlöf *The Legend of the Christmas Rose*
N°22 Charles Dickens *A Christmas Carol – Stave one*
N°23 Louisa May Alcott *A Christmas Dream*
N°24 H.C. Andersen *The Fir Tree*
N°25 Virginia Woolf *Kew Gardens*
N°26 James Joyce *The Boarding House*
N°27 Edith Wharton *The Quicksand*
N°28 Katherine Mansfield *The Garden Party*
N°29 Marcel Proust *The Melancholy Summer of Madame de Breyves*
N°30 Honoré de Balzac *A Street of Paris and Its Inhabitant*
N°31 Gustave Flaubert *The Legend of Saint Julian the Hospitaller*
N°32 Guy de Maupassant *Paul's Mistress*

*The Silver Mine*
Selma Lagerlöf

Translation by Velma Swanston Howard

NOVELLIX
— *stories to go* —

www.novellix.se

Originally published in Swedish in *Tösen från Stormyrtorpet och andra sagor* by Åhlén & Åkerlund, Sweden, 1913

Original title: *Silvergruvan*
Translation: Velma Swanston Howard

13

Design: Lisa Benk
Print: Livonia Print, Riga, 2025
ISBN: 978-91-7589-221-4

FSC
www.fsc.org
MIX
Paper | Supporting responsible forestry
FSC® C002795

KING GUSTAF THE THIRD was travelling through Dalecarlia. He was pressed for time, and all the way he wanted to drive like lightning. Although they drove with such speed that the horses were extended like stretched rubber bands and the coach cleared the turns on two wheels, the King poked his head out of the window and shouted to the postilion: "Why don't you go ahead? Do you think you are driving over eggs?"

Since they had to drive over poor country roads at such a mad pace, it would have been almost a miracle had the harness and wagon held together! And they didn't, either; for at the foot of a steep hill the pole broke—and there the King sat! The courtiers sprang from the coach and scolded the driver, but this did not lessen the damage done. There was no possibility of continuing the journey until the coach was mended.

They intimated to the King that he might step into one of the coaches in which the attendants were riding and drive up to the church. It was a Sunday, and the King might attend service to pass the time until the royal coach was ready.

The King accepted the proposal and drove toward the church. He had been travelling for hours through dark forest regions, but here it looked more cheerful, with fairly large meadows and villages, and with the Dal River gliding on, light and pretty, between thick rows of alder bushes.

But the King had ill-luck to this extent: the bell-ringer took up the recessional chant just as the King was stepping from the coach on the church knoll and the people were coming out from the service. But when they came walking past him, the King remained standing, with one foot in the wagon and the other on the footstep. He did not move from the spot—only stared at them. They were the finest lot of folk he had ever seen. All the men were above the average height, with intelligent and earnest faces, and the women were dignified and stately, with an air of Sabbath peace about them.

The whole of the preceding day the King had talked only of the desolate tracts he was passing through, and had said to his courtiers again and again,

"Now I am certainly driving through the very poorest part of my kingdom!" But now, when he saw the people, garbed in the picturesque dress of this section of the country, he forgot to think of their poverty; instead his heart warmed, and he remarked to himself: "The King of Sweden is not so badly off as his enemies think. So long as my subjects look like this, I shall probably be able to defend both my faith and my country."

He commanded the courtiers to make known to the people that the stranger who was standing amongst them was their King, and that they should gather around him, so he could talk to them.

And then the King made a speech to the people. He spoke from the high steps outside the vestry, and the narrow step upon which he stood is there even today.

The King gave an account of the sad plight in which the kingdom was placed. He said that the Swedes were threatened with war, both by Russians and Danes. Under ordinary circumstances it wouldn't be such a serious matter, but now the army was filled with traitors, and he did not dare depend upon it. Therefore there was no other course for him to pursue than to go himself into the country settlements and ask his subjects if they would be loyal to their King and help him with men and money, so he could save the Fatherland.

The peasants stood quietly while the King was speaking, and when he had finished they gave no sign either of approval or disapproval.

The King himself thought that he had spoken very well. The tears had sprung to his eyes several times while he was speaking. But when the peasants stood there all the while, troubled and undecided, and could not make up their minds to answer him, the King frowned and looked displeased.

The peasants understood that it was becoming monotonous for the King to wait, and finally one of them stepped out from the crowd.

"Now, you must know, King Gustaf, that we were not expecting a royal visit in the parish today," said the peasant, "and therefore we are not prepared to answer you at once. I advise you to go into the vestry and speak with our pastor, while we discuss among ourselves this matter which you have laid before us."

The King apprehended that a more satisfactory response was not to be had immediately, so he felt that it would be best for him to follow the peasant's advice.

When he came into the vestry, he found no one there but a man who looked like a peasant. He was tall and rugged, with big hands, toughened by labor, and he wore neither cassock nor collar, but leather breeches and a long white homespun coat, like all the other men.

He arose and bowed to the King when the latter entered.

"I thought I should find the parson in here," said the King.

The man grew somewhat red in the face. He thought it annoying to mention the fact that he was the parson of this parish, when he saw that the King had mistaken him for a peasant. "Yes," said he, "the parson is usually on hand in here."

The King dropped into a large armchair which stood in the vestry at that time, and which stands there today, looking exactly like itself, with this difference: the congregation has had a gilded crown attached to the back of it.

"Have you a good parson in this parish?" asked the King, who wanted to appear interested in the welfare of the peasants.

When the King questioned him in this manner, the parson felt that he couldn't possibly tell who he was. "It's better to let him go on believing that I'm only a peasant," thought he, and replied that the parson was good enough. He preached a pure and clear gospel and tried to live as he taught.

The King thought that this was a good commendation, but he had a sharp ear and marked a certain doubt in the tone. "You sound as if you were not quite satisfied with the parson," said the King.

"He's a bit arbitrary," said the man, thinking that if the King should find out later who he was, he would not think that the parson had been standing here and blowing his own horn, therefore he wished to come out with a little fault-finding also. "There are some, no doubt, who say the parson wants to be the only one to counsel and rule in this parish," he continued.

"Then, at all events, he has led and managed in the best possible way," said the King. He didn't like it that the peasant complained of one who was placed above him. "To me it appears as though good habits and old-time simplicity were the rule here."

"The people are good enough," said the curate, "but then they live in poverty and isolation. Human beings here would certainly be no better than others if this world's temptations came closer to them."

"But there's no fear of anything of the sort happening," said the King with a shrug.

He said nothing further, but began thrumming on the table with his fingers. He thought he had exchanged a sufficient number of gracious words with this peasant and wondered when the others would be ready with their answer.

"These peasants are not very eager to help their King," thought he. "If I only had my coach, I would drive away from them and their palaver!"

The pastor sat there troubled, debating with himself as to how he should decide an important matter which he must settle. He was beginning to feel happy because he had not told the King who he was. Now he felt that he could speak with him about matters which otherwise he could not have placed before him.

After a while the parson broke the silence and asked the King if it was an actual fact that enemies were upon them and that the kingdom was in danger.

The King thought this man ought to have sense enough not to trouble him further. He simply glared at him and said nothing.

"I ask because I was standing in here and could not hear very well," said the parson. "But if this is really the case, I want to say to you that the pastor of this congregation might perhaps be able to procure for the King as much money as he will need."

"I thought you said just now that everyone here was poor," said the King, thinking that the man didn't know what he was talking about.

"Yes, that is true," replied the rector, "and the parson has no more than any of the others. But if the King would condescend to listen to me for a moment, I will explain how the pastor happens to have the power to help him."

"You may speak," said the King. "You seem to find it easier to get the words past your lips than your friends and neighbors out there, who never will be ready with what they have to tell me."

"It is not so easy to reply to the King! I'm afraid that, in the end, it will be the parson who must undertake this on behalf of the others."

The King crossed his legs, folded his arms, and let his head sink down on his breast. "You may begin now," he said in the tone of one already asleep.

"Once upon a time there were five men from this parish who were out on a moose hunt," began the clergyman. "One of them was the parson of whom we are speaking. Two of the others were soldiers, named Olaf and Eric Svärd; the fourth man was the innkeeper in this settlement, and the fifth was a peasant named Israel Per Persson."

"Don't go to the trouble of mentioning so many names," muttered the King, letting his head droop to one side.

"Those men were good hunters," continued the parson, "who usually had luck with them; but that day they had wandered long and far without getting anything. Finally they gave up the hunt altogether and sat down on the ground to talk. They said there was not a spot in the whole forest fit for cultivation; all of it was only mountain and swamp land. 'Our Lord has not done right by us in giving us such a poor land to live in,' said one. 'In other localities people can get riches for themselves in abundance, but here, with all our toil and drudgery, we can scarcely get our daily bread'."

The pastor paused a moment, as if uncertain that the King heard him, but the latter moved his little finger to show that he was awake.

"Just as the hunters were discussing this matter, the parson saw something that glittered at the base of the mountain, where he had kicked away a moss-tuft. 'This is a queer mountain,' he thought, as he kicked off another moss-tuft. He picked up a shiver of stone that came with the moss and which shone exactly like the other. 'It can't be possible that this stuff is lead,' said he. Then the others sprang up and scraped away the turf with the butt-end of their rifles. When they did this, they saw plainly that a broad vein of ore followed the mountain. 'What do you think this might be?' asked the parson. The men chipped off bits of stone and bit into them. 'It must be lead, or zinc at least,' said they. 'And the whole mountain is full of it,' added the innkeeper."

When the parson had got thus far in his narrative, the King's head was seen to straighten up a little and one eye opened. "Do you know if any of those persons knew anything about ore and minerals?" he asked.

"They did not," replied the parson.

Then the King's head sank and both eyes closed.

"The clergyman and his companions were very happy," continued the speaker, without letting himself be disturbed by the King's indifference; "they fancied that now they had found that which would give them and their descendants wealth. 'I'll never have to do any more work,' said one. 'Now I can afford to do nothing at all the whole week through, and on Sundays I shall drive to church in a golden chariot!' They were otherwise sensible men, but the great find had gone to their heads and they talked like children. Still they had enough presence of mind to put back the moss-tufts and conceal the vein of ore. Then they carefully noted the place where it was, and went home. Before they parted company, they agreed that the parson should travel to Falun and ask the mining expert what kind of ore this was. He was to return as soon as possible, and until then they promised one another on oath not to reveal to a single soul where the ore was to be found."

The King's head was raised again a trifle, but he did not interrupt the speaker with a word. It appeared as though he was beginning to believe that the man actually had something of importance he wished to say to him, since he didn't allow himself to be disturbed by his indifference.

"Then the parson departed with a few samples of ore in his pocket. He was just as happy in the thought of becoming rich as the others were. He was thinking of rebuilding the parsonage, which at present was no better than a peasant's cottage, and then he would marry a dean's daughter whom he liked. He had thought that he might have to wait for her many years! He was poor and obscure and knew that it would be a long while before he should get any post that would enable him to marry.

The parson drove over to Falun in two days, and there he had to wait another whole day because the mining expert was away. Finally, he ran across him and showed him the bits of ore. The mining expert took them in his hand. He looked at them first, then at the parson. The parson related how he had found them in a mountain at home in his parish, and wondered if it might not be lead.

'No, it's not lead,' said the mining expert.

'Perhaps it is zinc, then?' asked the parson.

'Nor is it zinc,' said the mineralogist.

The parson thought that all the hope within him sank. He had not been so depressed in many a long day.

'Have you many stones like these in your parish?' asked the mineralogist.

'We have a whole mountain full,' said the parson.

Then the mineralogist came up closer, slapped the parson on the shoulder, and said, 'Let us see that you make such good use of this that it will prove a blessing both to yourselves and to the country, for this is silver.'

'Indeed?' said the parson, feeling his way. 'So it is silver!'

The mineralogist began telling him how he should go to work to get legal rights to the mine and gave him many valuable suggestions; but the parson stood there dazed and didn't listen to what he was saying. He was only thinking of how wonderful it was that at home in his poor parish stood a whole mountain of silver ore, waiting for him."

The King raised his head so suddenly that the parson stopped short in his narrative. "It turned out, of course, that when he got home and began working the mine, he saw that the mineralogist had only been fooling him," said the King.

"Oh, no, the mineralogist had not fooled him," said the parson.

"You may continue," said the King, as he settled himself more comfortably in the chair to listen.

"When the parson was at home again and was driving through the parish," continued the clergyman, "he thought that first of all he should inform his partners of the value of their find. And as he drove alongside the innkeeper Sten Stensson's place, he intended to drive up to the house to tell him they had found silver. But when he stopped outside the gate, he noticed that a broad path of evergreen was strewn all the way up to the doorstep.

'Who has died in this place?' asked the parson of a boy who stood leaning against the fence.

'The innkeeper himself,' answered the boy. Then he let the clergyman know that the innkeeper had drunk himself full every day for a week. 'Oh, so much brandy, so much brandy has been drunk here!'

'How can that be?' asked the parson. 'The innkeeper used never to drink himself full.'

'Oh,' said the boy, 'he drank because he said he had found a mine. He was very rich. He should never have to do anything now but drink, he said.

Last night he drove off, full as he was, and the wagon turned over and he was killed.'

When the parson heard this, he drove homeward. He was distressed over what he had heard. He had come back so happy, rejoicing because he could tell the great good news.

When the parson had driven a few paces, he saw Israel Per Persson walking along. He looked about as usual, and the parson thought it was well that fortune had not gone to his head too. Him he would cheer at once with the news that he was a rich man.

'Good day!' said Per Persson. 'Do you come from Falun now?'

'I do,' said the parson. 'And now I must tell you that it has turned out even better than we had imagined. The mineralogist said it was silver ore that we had found.'

That instant Per Persson looked as though the ground under him had opened! 'What are you saying, what are you saying? Is it silver?'

'Yes,' answered the parson. 'We'll all be rich men now, all of us, and can live like gentlemen.'

'Oh, is it silver!' said Per Persson once again, looking more and more mournful.

'Why, of course it is silver,' replied the parson. 'You mustn't think that I want to deceive you. You mustn't be afraid of being happy.'

'Happy!' said Per Persson. 'Should I be happy? I believed it was only glitter that we had found, so I thought it would be better to take the certain for the uncertain: I have sold my share in the mine to Olaf Svärd for a hundred dollars.' He was desperate, and when the parson drove away from him, he stood on the highway and wept.

When the clergyman got back to his home, he sent a servant to Olaf Svärd and his brother to tell them that it was silver they had found. He thought that he had had quite enough of driving around and spreading the good news.

But in the evening, when the parson sat alone, his joy asserted itself again. He went out in the darkness and stood on a hillock upon which he contemplated building the new parsonage. It should be imposing, of course, as fine as a bishop's palace. He stood out there long that night; nor did he content himself with rebuilding the parsonage! It occurred to him that, since there were such riches to be found in the parish, throngs of people would pour in and, finally, a whole city would be built around the mine. And then he would have to erect a new church in place of the old one. Towards this object a large portion of his wealth would probably go. And he was not content with this, either, but fancied that when his church was ready, the King and many bishops would come to the dedication. Then the King would be pleased with the church, but he would remark that there was no place where a king might put up, and then he would have to erect a castle in the new city."

Just then one of the King's courtiers opened the door of the vestry and announced that the big royal coach was mended.

At the first moment the King was ready to withdraw, but on second thought he changed his mind. "You may tell your story to the end," he said to the parson. "But you can hurry it a bit. We know all about how the man thought and dreamed. We want to know how he acted."

"But while the parson was still lost in his dreams," continued the clergyman, "word came to him that Israel Per Persson had made away with himself. He had not been able to bear the disappointment of having sold his share in the mine. He had thought, no doubt, that he could not endure to go about every day seeing another enjoying the wealth that might have been his."

The King straightened up a little. He kept both eyes open. "Upon my word," he said, "if I had been that parson, I should have had enough of the mine!"

"The King is a rich man," said the parson. "He

has quite enough, at all events. It is not the same thing with a poor curate who possesses nothing. The unhappy wretch thought instead, when he saw that God's blessing was not with his enterprise: 'I will dream no more of bringing glory and profit to myself with these riches; but I can't let the silver lie buried in the earth! I must take it out, for the benefit of the poor and needy. I will work the mine, to put the whole parish on its feet.'

So one day the parson went out to see Olaf Svärd, to ask him and his brother as to what should be done immediately with the silver mountain. When he came in the vicinity of the barracks, he met a cart surrounded by armed peasants, and in the cart sat a man with his hands tied behind him and a rope around his ankles.

When the parson passed by, the cart stopped, and he had time to regard the prisoner, whose head was tied up so it wasn't casy to see who he was. But the parson thought he recognized Olaf Svärd. He heard the prisoner beg those who guarded him to let him speak a few words with the parson.

The parson drew nearer, and the prisoner turned toward him. 'You will soon be the only one who knows where the silver mine is,' said Olaf.

'What are you saying, Olaf?' asked the parson.

'Well, you see, parson, since we have learned that it was a silver mine we had found, my brother and I could no longer be as good friends as before. We were continually quarrelling. Last night we got into a controversy over which one of us five it was who first discovered the mine. It ended in strife between us, and we came to blows. I have killed my brother and he has left me with a souvenir across the forehead to remember him by. I must hang now, and then you will be the only one who knows anything about the mine; therefore I wish to ask something of you.'

'Speak out!' said the parson. 'I'll do what I can for you.'

'You know that I am leaving several little children behind me,' began the soldier, but the parson interrupted him.

'As regards this, you can rest easy. That which comes to your share in the mine, they shall have, exactly as if you yourself were living.'

'No,' said Olaf Svärd, 'it was another thing I wanted to ask of you. Don't let them have any portion of that which comes from the mine!'

The parson staggered back a step. He stood there dumb and could not answer.

'If you do not promise me this, I cannot die in peace,' said the prisoner.

'Yes,' said the parson slowly and painfully. 'I promise you what you ask of me.'

Thereupon the murderer was taken away, and the parson stood on the highway thinking how he should keep the promise he had given him. On the way home he thought of the wealth which he had been so happy over. But if it really were true that the people in this community could not stand riches?—Already four were ruined, who hitherto had been dignified and excellent men. He seemed to see the whole community before him, and he pictured to himself how this silver mine would destroy one after another. Was it befitting that he, who had been appointed to watch over these poor human beings' souls, should let loose upon them that which would be their destruction?"

All of a sudden the King sat bolt upright in his chair. "I declare!" said he, "you'll make me understand that a parson in this isolated settlement must be every inch a man."

"Nor was it enough with what had already happened," continued the parson, "for as soon as the news about the mine spread among the parishioners, they stopped working and went about in idleness, waiting for the time when great riches should pour in on them. All the ne'er-do-wells there were in this section streamed in, and drunkenness and fighting were what the parson heard talked of continually. A lot of people did nothing but tramp round in the forest searching for the mine, and the parson marked that as soon as he left the house people followed him stealthily to find out if he wasn't going to the silver mountain and to steal the secret from him.

When matters were come to this pass, the parson called the peasants together to vote. To start with, he reminded them of all the misfortunes which the discovery of the mountain had brought upon them, and he asked them if they were going to let themselves be ruined or if they would save themselves. Then he told them that they must not expect him, who was their spiritual adviser, to help on their destruction. Now he had decided not to reveal to anyone where the silver mine was, and never would he himself take riches from it. And then he asked the peasants how they would have it henceforth. If they wished to continue their search for the mine and wait upon riches, then he would go so far away that not a hearsay of their misery could reach him; but if they would give up thinking about the silver mine and be as heretofore, he would remain with them. 'Whichever way you may choose,' said the parson, 'remember this, that from me no one shall ever know anything about the silver mountain!'"

"Well," said the King, "how did they decide?"

"They did as their pastor wished," said the parson. "They understood that he meant well by them when he wanted to remain poor for their sakes. And they commissioned him to go to the forest and conceal the vein of ore with evergreen and stone, so that no one would be able to find it—neither they themselves nor their posterity."

"And ever since the parson has been living here just as poor as the rest?"

"Yes," answered the curate, "he has lived here just as poor as the rest."

"He has married, of course, and built himself a new parsonage?" said the King.

"No, he couldn't afford to marry, and he lives in the old cabin."

"It's a pretty story that you have told me," said the King. After a few seconds he resumed: "Was it of the silver mountain that you were thinking when you said that the parson here would be able to procure for me as much money as I need?"

"Yes," said the other.

"But I can't put the thumb-screws on him," said the King. "Or how would you that I should get such a man to show me the mountain—a man who has renounced his sweetheart and all the allurements of life?"

"Oh, that's a different matter," said the parson. "But if it's the Fatherland that is in need of the fortune, he will probably give in."

"Will you answer for that?" asked the King.

"Yes, that I will answer for," said the clergyman.

"Doesn't he care, then, what becomes of his parishioners?"

"That can rest in God's hand."

The King rose from the chair and walked over to the window. He stood for a moment and looked upon the group of people outside. The longer he looked, the clearer his large eyes shone, and his figure seemed to grow. "You may greet the pastor of this congregation, and say that for Sweden's King there is no sight more beautiful than to see a people such as this!"

Then the King turned from the window and looked at the clergyman. He began to smile. "Is it true that the pastor of this parish is so poor that he removes his black clothes as soon as the service is over and dresses himself like a peasant?" asked the King.

"Yes, so poor is he," said the curate, and a crimson flush leaped into his rough-hewn face.

The King went back to the window. One could

see that he was in his best mood. All that was noble and great within him had been quickened into life. "You must let that mine lie in peace," said the King. "Inasmuch as you have labored and starved a lifetime to make this people such as you would have it, you may keep it as it is."

"But if the kingdom is in danger?" said the parson.

"The kingdom is better served with men than with money," remarked the King. When he had said this, he bade the clergyman farewell and went out from the vestry.

Without stood the group of people, as quiet and taciturn as they were when he went in. As the King came down the steps, a peasant stepped up to him.

"Have you had a talk with our pastor?" said the peasant.

"Yes," said the King. "I have talked with him."

"Then of course you have our answer?" said the peasant. "We asked you to go in and talk with our parson, that he might give you an answer from us."

"I have the answer," said the King.

SHORT STORIES PUBLISHED BY NOVELLIX

N°1 Virginia Woolf *Lappin and Lapinova*
N°2 D.H. Lawrence *Sun*
N°3 Katherine Mansfield *Bliss*
N°4 Charles Dickens *Horatio Sparkins*
N°5 Astrid Lindgren *Most Beloved Sister & Mirabelle*
N°6 August Strindberg *Frictions*
N°7 Selma Lagerlöf *The Silver Mine*
N°8 Stig Dagerman *Sleet*
N°9 Håkan Nesser *How I Spend My Days and My Nights*
N°10 Karin Tidbeck *Anywhere Out of the World*
N°11 Arne Dahl *Migraine*
N°12 Henning Mankell *The Man on the Beach*
N°13 Oscar Wilde *The Nightinggale and the Rose...*
N°14 Mary Shelley *The Trial of Love*
N°15 Leo Tolstoy *After the Dance*
N°16 Virginia Woolf *The Legacy*
N°17 Karen Blixen *The Pearls*
N°18 Henrik Pontoppidan *The Grim Reaper*
N°19 Herman Bang *Irene Holm*
N°20 H.C. Andersen *Little Claus and Big Claus*
N°21 Selma Lagerlöf *The Legend of the Christmas Rose*
N°22 Charles Dickens *A Christmas Carol – Stave one*
N°23 Louisa May Alcott *A Christmas Dream*
N°24 H.C. Andersen *The Fir Tree*
N°25 Virginia Woolf *Kew Gardens*
N°26 James Joyce *The Boarding House*
N°27 Edith Wharton *The Quicksand*
N°28 Katherine Mansfield *The Garden Party*
N°29 Marcel Proust *The Melancholy Summer of Madame de Breyves*
N°30 Honoré de Balzac *A Street of Paris and Its Inhabitant*
N°31 Gustave Flaubert *The Legend of Saint Julian the Hospitaller*
N°32 Guy de Maupassant *Paul's Mistress*

*Ella Breaks Free*

Karin Boye

Translated by Alexei Liss

NOVELLIX
— stories to go —

www.novellix.com

Originally published in Swedish in the short story collection *Ur funktion*, Albert Bonniers förlag, Sweden, 1940

Original title: *Ella gör sig fri* Translation: Alexei Liss

Published by Novellix, Stockholm, 2024

2

Cover image: Shutterstock.com Cover design: Hanna Hallin
Livonia Print, Riga, 2025
ISBN: 978-91-7589-663-2

FSC
www.fsc.org
MIX
Paper | Supporting responsible forestry
FSC® C002795

"ANYTHING – I CAN ENDURE almost anything," Ella uttered in a voice that was tired to the brink of death. "But that he also despises me is the worst thing of all. It makes everything utterly meaningless."

The other woman's cornflower-blue eyes widened with indignation.

"No, really, that's the last straw!" she exclaimed. "I have rarely heard anything as preposterous. 'Despises' you!"

The two women faced each other across the table by the window. The one who lived there was pale and slender, with dark hair neatly parted over a well-shaped head, resting her hands on a shirt in need of mending in her lap. Her hands were not the deft, delicate hands of an embroiderer; rather, they were sinewy and roughened, coarsened by a habit of attending to whatever needed to be done. The visitor wore a hat and a blue dress. Her poised posture, extending all the way up to her bright, frizzy hair, suggested a woman of independence.

"You should know," said the independent woman, "that Arvid flirts with others."

"I don't need you to tell me that. Of course he flirts with others; he always has. But that doesn't particularly bother me."

There was a moment's silence.

"And not only that – but it's also how he makes you support him. You already have your job, and then he makes you take on all that extra work so he can go on drinking and God knows what else!"

Ella only smiled bitterly.

"If I were you, I would have kicked him out a long time ago! Why should poets, of all people, be allowed to act however they want? While I hold Arvid's talents in high regard, I consider him no genius, and even if he were, couldn't he behave like a decent human being? And then he despises you on top of it all! Have you simply given up?"

Ella made a weary gesture with her head.

"Imagine how good your life would be without him holding you back. You have your livelihood; just think how far it would stretch if you were on your own. You would have time for leisure and plenty of time to travel. Imagine what a life you could make for yourself!"

Plenty more was said, with Astrid leading the conversation. She fussed and urged her to protest without allowing herself to feel disheartened by the lack of enthusiasm she received in response. Ella didn't even so much as grumble. She merely sighed and smiled bitterly. When it was finally time for Astrid to leave, she turned around in the doorway to reaffirm her opinion:

"I don't know if you're a fool or a saint – perhaps both – but one thing is for sure: that man should thank his creator for having you as his wife. What a shame you ended up with a bastard like Arvid. He doesn't deserve you."

Ella returned to her shirt with a smile on her face, though it was not quite the same bitter and acquiescent smile as before. It was soft and grateful, as if she had been given a small reward for her unwavering perseverance after all. Her thoughts drifted to the image of her mother, the way she was seated in her large chair the day before when Ella had visited her: slight and worn by the sorrows of life and the aches of old age, but with lucid eyes and with the same stern lines around her mouth as when Ella was a young girl. Yes, she had always been stern, both towards herself and others. "We must live with the consequences of our choices," she used to say. She had certainly been burdened with the consequences of her choices her entire life, poor mother. As a child, Ella had never quite understood *what* was wrong with her father, only *that* there was something wrong. It was obvious that her mother knew, and it was obvious that her father also knew. His entire demeanour confirmed it. He had once been cheerful and kind, always spreading joy, but his spark had gradually faded. Ella had the feeling that he unsuccessfully tried hiding in the background. Her mother's sharp eyes penetrated everything concealed, revealing all that was wrong, even though she never uttered a single word. Later on, Ella had the impression that her father was the sort of person others would smirk at – not with kindness but with contempt – and in truth, she often saw that smirk on her mother's lips. It was unclear how it had reached this point, but she feared nothing as much as she feared that smirk and would rather endure anything than be subjected to it. As Ella and her siblings were all afraid of the small, silent and stern woman who authoritatively wielded her supercilious smile, they abided by their mother's with embarrassing diligence. It was only when Ella studied towards her confirmation that a striking incident proved her mother right even more conspicuously. This was when her father returned home drunk. Although it hadn't happened before, it was somehow what they had been waiting for. She looked back on the persistent tension between her parents as if it were some sort of prosecution, in which allegations and defence were shrouded in an impenetrable darkness, though eventually, through years of perseverance, the plaintiff had managed to obtain decisive evidence in her favour. Father was guilty as charged. Even though he had already been morally guilty for a long time, he could now be said to be legally culpable too.

The only time Ella had seriously defied her mother's wishes was when she married Arvid, which had occurred in a state of exhilaration, and now she would be unable to explain how she had found the nerve for such an act of rebellion. By the time the exhilaration had faded and the tedium of daily life had begun, she was horrified to discover that, just as for her parents, an invisible ledger lay before them with a separate column for credit and debit for them each. Which one of them would be proven right, and which one would be proven wrong? She found that nothing was more important to her than bringing the ledger to a favourable conclusion for herself, especially since her mother had warned her from the start. Ella didn't want to be someone who shirked her duties. "We must live with the consequences of our choices."

She let the shirt rest in her lap while snippets from her childhood and youth passed her by, melding into a grey, indiscernible mesh. There had almost always been a heavy burden to bear – almost always some unpleasant responsibility to fulfil. But even that had been a relief, knowing that her mother liked, or at least did not dislike, what she did. In this way, she had followed all her children through their lives. Even when she wasn't near, the vivid and pervasive image of her was always present, and after death, she would certainly continue to dictate their actions down to the last detail, just as she had when they were children. "Naturally, you should do as you wish. You know what I think." Naturally. And so, their mother's wishes were followed.

It was already late in the day when she heard the sound of jangling keys, the door open, and Arvid walk in. He came up to where Ella was seated and stood watching her sew. She made no acknowledgment of his presence, only sewing slightly faster with a sardonic smile on her lips, knowing that she was gathering ammunition against the sins of someone other than herself.

"You go ahead," Arvid said. "Keep at it until I feel ashamed and repent of my sinful ways, but I can assure you that there won't be enough thread to see it through." Whistling, he removed his jacket and put on his old work coat. He took a seat by the typewriter beside the other window and began revising the short story he had finished. But it wasn't long until he jumped up and slammed his fist against the table.

"Deceitful shrew!" he screamed furiously. "The whole room is poisoned, disgusting – I can't work in this atmosphere."

"Would you like me to sit in the pantry and mend your shirts?" Ella asked frostily.

"I would like it if you threw yourself in the slop

bucket so I wouldn't have to see you!" he replied, his voice laced with despair. "And how cruel he is, that vile man! Compared to little Ella, who prefers methods of slow suffocation, being the refined and delicate person that she is!"

"Would you like dinner?" Ella asked as she rose from her seat.

"Not if you're the cook! I'd rather starve to death! Besides, I've already eaten."

"Then I hope you will excuse me for having a sandwich," Ella said. "I had, as a matter of fact, been waiting to have dinner with you."

"You're excused!" he hissed as he sat back at the typewriter while she left to grab a bite to eat.

"I am working extra tonight, so I will need to leave soon," she said. This was entirely true – she would never allow herself to lie.

"Now you probably expect me to fall to my knees in gratitude for your sacrifice and for working yourself to exhaustion for my sake, etcetera, etcetera," he retorted angrily. "But I won't! You don't have an altruistic impulse within you. You only want to kill me with guilt."

"How can you!" she mumbled in despair as she prepared to leave.

It was nine o'clock by the time she walked home through the dimly lit streets. Fatigue and nightfall lulled her into a tender state of half-sleep, while the memories that had flowed abundantly in the morning continued to stream. But now they were reminiscences of a different sort, ones that had eluded her earlier in the day. These were images of her first evenings together with Arvid. It was September, dark like now, but warmer. They had walked along the outskirts of the city, past modern developments and allotments where the last dahlias bloomed in the light of lanterns. The temperate darkness, her tiredness, and the unfamiliar surroundings had soothed her into a dreamlike state, much like how she felt now. The strange man beside her had radiated with life; he was someone different and was leading her into something new. The impressions were new, and so was the world. The green-painted trellises encircling the allotment cottages – overgrown with the yellowed leaves of runner beans, the shadows that deepened under the dim and intermittent lampposts, the damp scent of impending autumn – everything breathed of a new and wonderful adventure. She was on the verge of breaking free from everything, daring to venture into an ocean of unknown delight. Tonight, these memories overwhelmed her with particular acrimony – to think that all those promises would wither into petty-mindedness and conflict, that Arvid would not measure up … And at the same time, a fierce longing welled up in her. To sail away from shore once again, to be new, to be free, to start afresh, to be a blank page …

"This has gone too far," she muttered to herself in a grave tone. "Surely one is not obliged to endure just about anything?"

Deeper inside, she reflected, with relief, that maybe – just maybe – a new form of freedom awaited her.

Instead of going straight home, she ascended the small, steep street where her mother lived. Where else would she go? She felt that she had reached a crossroads. Who else could help her other than the person who was her constant conscience? She would lay bare the contents of her entire ledger and let her mother judge for herself if the breaking point had been reached. If she were to say: "Not yet!" then she had not fulfilled her duty until the end, and she would return home and stay there. But if she said: "That's enough!" then she would finally know that she could surrender her burden. The street angled steeply upward, but she walked lightly since she was going towards the one person who would be able to put an end to her doubts – the only one whose judgement she was willing to submit to – the one whose eyes had been on her all her life.

And so, she arrived. Given the hour of the night, the front door was closed, but seeing that the light in the window remained lit, she dared to knock. The elderly woman opened the window and peered out into the darkness. Slowly, she recognised her daughter and handed her the key, which she used to open the door, quietly entering the small, old-fashioned room where she took a seat in her usual corner by the tiled stove. Her mother had not yet made the bed; she had been crocheting when she was interrupted by her daughter's knock.

Now, as they sat facing each other, she put down her handiwork and gazed at her daughter with clear eyes. Ella withstood the gaze. Her soul was tormented and she yearned for nothing more than guidance and support for how to act, so the more those eyes saw, the better. But for the first time in her life, she had the feeling that their clarity betrayed her, that they stared at something beyond what was in the room, beyond herself, and out at something that occupied them more.

"I've been sitting here thinking about your childhood," her mother said before Ella had a chance to share her troubles. "No, I can't say your genes were entirely good. But how could they have been? It doesn't matter if a mother resolves to perfectly raise her children; they all have two parents, after all. Yes, even you, little Ella. You always wanted the largest cookie for yourself, but I tried to correct that. I taught you from the very start that this was improper, and you changed for your mother's sake. Then, I will never forget when Jan came home using dirty words he had learned at school. That evening, I cried in shame of my own child. But this, too, I put an end to through patience and resolve. My will was strong and that was crucial. I fought for my children like a lioness, and in the end, emerged victorious. Your mother's legacy took precedence, though this was only and entirely thanks to my own relentless and unwavering effort. Where would you be without that resolve?"

Ella watched her mother's eyes rummage through the years in search of triumphs to be proud of and was suddenly overcome with compassion for the old woman. To dwell on the past like that! Did she constantly need to reassure herself that she had been useful, that she could be proud, and that ultimately, she was a good person? It was touching, but in the way that fragility is touching. She had hoped to find a strong person – someone who could see through her child and identify what she needed – but this old woman, with her handiwork in her lap, was clearly not able to see through her. She couldn't even properly see her because she was preoccupied with herself. This was something Ella had not seen before. Then again, she had never before sought her help in such a helpless way.

Now the old woman's voice turned sour. "And I never had any help; no, no help at all. It fell on me to help everyone, but no one ever helped me. I was all alone and forced to toil away, and now I sit here exhausted. But at least I have done right by myself – I wish everyone could say as much." Ella felt almost ashamed that she was sitting there thinking about herself. Yet so was her mother. And with her mother so focused on her own righteousness and grievances she would never dare come forward with her own concerns. It would serve no purpose. Her idol had abandoned her. Worse still, her idol had forever fallen from her pedestal and transformed into a weak, frail human being.

Ella suddenly felt that she was all alone in the world. The old woman, of whom she had been so afraid and so eager to please, had suddenly withdrawn into indifference, and her words no longer held the power to either frighten or console. How strange to stand in the centre of the world and be all alone.

Had she really come to hear and then follow her mother's advice? Why? She was on her own. Nobody could tell her, "You're duty-bound to persevere," just as no one could say, "I release you from your duties." It had to be her own decision. There was no need to ask anyone else.

For a while longer, she listened half-heartedly to the old woman's complaints and self-praise. Then she fleetingly kissed her mother's cheek – a kiss of weary compassion – and returned home filled with loneliness and the freedom to act as she saw fit.

Arvid, who was lying on the ottoman peacefully reading a book, looked up and nodded as she entered. In truth, she would have been indifferent, no matter the state she found him in. What had to be said needed to be said. "Arvid," she said calmly, taking a seat at the end of the ottoman. "I want a divorce."

He set the book aside but remained reclined, looking at her. There was none of the usual mockery in his gaze – he saw that she was serious.

"Yes," he said. "Yes, I understand that."

He said nothing more, merely lying there, staring in silence with a serious expression on his face. Nor did she say anything more but went into the bedroom and undressed. After a while, she heard the sound of him making his bed on the ottoman.

Breakfast the next morning was silent and brief. After eating, they settled down with their cigarettes for a serious conversation.

"So, I suppose we're getting divorced," Arvid said. "I realise that I have behaved quite poorly. In fact, I realise just how much you mean to me."

"Don't worry about all that," Ella said, suddenly generous now that she would soon break free. "It is just that it can't go on."

"No – no, I understand!" he agreed, with his voice so filled with considerate regret and supressed unease that it brought tears to her eyes. One of Arvid's more enchanting traits had always been his sudden and sincere humility whenever he became aware of the harm he had caused and his ability to view the situation from the other person's perspective. In this moment, she once again saw what she had lately been unable to fathom: why she had once fallen so madly in love with this person, who, in certain ways, couldn't even be considered a grown-up.

"Before we part ways," he said, taking her hand, "there's something I want to tell you. All that talk about how disgusting you are, how much I despised you and so on, it wasn't at all true. Not at its core. You could certainly be difficult at times, mean in a particularly shrewd and deceitful manner – forgive me, but it's true. Though deep down, I always knew who you were. And I cared for you."

He swallowed and fell silent. She listened to him as if he were a stranger. Only a day ago, his words would have troubled her – at once both wounding her and applying ointment to her open sores. But overnight, all her wounds had scarred, and now no new ones would be formed. Whether he despised her or adored her no longer mattered. She was alone.

"You probably don't know what it has meant to me that you've been here for me all these years," he continued. "I think I would have hit rock-bottom without you."

The last part sounded almost like a whisper. Ella waited, expecting him to plead for her to stay and continue to support him in the future.

"I didn't want you to leave believing that I truly meant all those things I said," he said after a while. "You should know how I really felt."

He rose to his feet and began pacing around the room. Meanwhile, he described the plans he had for himself: first he would stay with a good friend who lived in another part of town, then look for an apartment in a more affordable suburb. Given that lately they had been living on her income, it was obvious that she would be the one to keep their home.

Had she not felt so alone – had she remained in her previous state of aggravation, seeking insults to note down in her ledger, finding them all over the place – then she would surely have thought she heard a veiled sense of relief in his voice, an impolite eagerness to shed himself of the past that would have wounded her deeply. But now, she sat like a stranger and heard that he was masking his fear of being alone, and only so as not to load her with yet another burden. In many ways, this man was a dubious figure, but in other ways, he was a good person – in a completely different, deeper, and less calculating way than she had ever been.

Nonetheless, faced with what he didn't voice, filled her with concern. He was absolutely right that, without her, he would have sunk to the bottom. But it was not really that she had endeavoured to keep him afloat. Rather, it was that she had driven him away with her insufferable righteousness and unbearable patience, and he had kept himself afloat with thoughts of her. What if she now let him go? But of course, this was not the way to think; an adult must stand on his own two feet. She had no obligation to nanny a grown man. He began gathering his belongings. Although he didn't want to take much, only the essentials, it took a long time for him to sort through his things. The way he crammed them into his suitcase was awful. If only she could help him. However, he would surely dislike that, construing it as condescending, now when he needed to feel free and independent.

She concluded with cutting certainty that he would hit rock-bottom no matter what. Not in moral terms; no matter where he found himself, his ambition as a poet would keep him sustained on the level where bourgeois conceptions of achievement like her mother's couldn't suffice. But practically and financially he would plummet. The consequences became clear to her in that instant: the difficulties caused, the obstacles it would create for his work, and how much time he would waste in a futile struggle. His poetical aspirations would die on that hill. He needed her, even if he would not express it.

As if he had sensed a warmer breeze in the air, he suddenly turned and looked at her. His gaze met hers, beseeching and lost. He then approached and took her hands in his, while he said calmly and softly with downcast eyes: "Ella, if I truly, truly resolve to become a different person, do you think we could try to stay together just a little while longer?"

She didn't respond, and he let go of her hands and turned the other way.

"Oh well," he said with resignation. "I suppose I have treated you too poorly. You can't, I understand. Don't think I don't understand that."

In that moment, when he asked her to stay, her anguish became unbearable. Was he trying to force her to be merciful?

She knew all about his attempts at improvement. A short time would pass before his old spiteful ways would resurface again. Right now, he was saying how much he respected her, but in a month, he would unleash his harshest contempt. And why should those hurtful words not be taken to be as sincere as the kind ones he was speaking now? He meant them all! And she was free. She didn't care what he thought. He couldn't coerce her into leniency, which, besides, would have been nothing more than a gesture of kindness.

And yet, she smiled! What would it actually matter if he despised her once more or hurled hurtful words her way? He was not an adult. It would not shake her. She was about to laugh at herself for how much she had clung to what he said or did not say about her. If she let him stay now, it would only be because she didn't wish for him to be dragged down more than necessary; because she didn't want his work hampered by a loneliness he could not bear; because she didn't want him to be ensnared in endless trivial concerns. What he thought of her didn't matter. Here she was still, like a stranger, a spectator, knowing very well that this man, who was so weak and so venerable, was much too dear for her to want to interpret his faults as a personal insult.

"*Do* you really want to stay with me?" she asked, smiling.

He approached her, cravingly absorbing the expression on her face.

"Of course I do …"

"Then stay, Arvid, and let us start afresh – for the hundredth time."

He embraced her quietly, tightly and gratefully. It would not be the hundredth time; it would be *a different time*, he promised himself. As he had done before.

But she sat there thinking that from her perspective it was the very first time. Because she was on her own, alone and free. Perhaps that's why she felt closer to him than ever before. In a distant and somewhat comical contemplation, she thought: "Poor mother, tomorrow she will scold Arvid as usual and admonish me, thinking that everything is the same as before. She will never suspect that everything has changed."

SHORT STORIES PUBLISHED BY NOVELLIX

N°1 Virginia Woolf *Lappin and Lapinova*
N°2 D.H. Lawrence *Sun*
N°3 Katherine Mansfield *Bliss*
N°4 Charles Dickens *Horatio Sparkins*
N°5 Astrid Lindgren *Most Beloved Sister & Mirabelle*
N°6 August Strindberg *Frictions*
N°7 Selma Lagerlöf *The Silver Mine*
N°8 Stig Dagerman *Sleet*
N°9 Håkan Nesser *How I Spend My Days and My Nights*
N°10 Karin Tidbeck *Anywhere Out of the World*
N°11 Arne Dahl *Migraine*
N°12 Henning Mankell *The Man on the Beach*
N°13 Oscar Wilde *The Nightinggale and the Rose...*
N°14 Mary Shelley *The Trial of Love*
N°15 Leo Tolstoy *After the Dance*
N°16 Virginia Woolf *The Legacy*
N°17 Karen Blixen *The Pearls*
N°18 Henrik Pontoppidan *The Grim Reaper*
N°19 Herman Bang *Irene Holm*
N°20 H.C. Andersen *Little Claus and Big Claus*
N°21 Selma Lagerlöf *The Legend of the Christmas Rose*
N°22 Charles Dickens *A Christmas Carol – Stave one*
N°23 Louisa May Alcott *A Christmas Dream*
N°24 H.C. Andersen *The Fir Tree*
N°25 Virginia Woolf *Kew Gardens*
N°26 James Joyce *The Boarding House*
N°27 Edith Wharton *The Quicksand*
N°28 Katherine Mansfield *The Garden Party*
N°29 Marcel Proust *The Melancholy Summer of Madame de Breyves*
N°30 Honoré de Balzac *A Street of Paris and Its Inhabitant*
N°31 Gustave Flaubert *The Legend of Saint Julian the Hospitaller*
N°32 Guy de Maupassant *Paul's Mistress*